*The Absent Color* is an authentic miracle: deep philosophical insights clearly rendered in poetic language. It is not versified philosophy but a true *thinking* in the form of poems. It shatters you. Like a sharp razor, it cuts deep into your skin. But it is a strangely pleasurable pain, a pain which makes you stronger because it compels you to confront the truth—in its most traumatic dimension.
**Slavoj Žižek**, philosopher

These poems come in a singular voice—defiant, ironic, suddenly tender, often within a single poem. A voice which has read everyone, but imitates no one. A/nil's English is his own and the unexpected syntax, the often radical image making, forces us to go slowly, to retrace our steps. That is the only way to experience the universe of A/nil's poems, which is layered, manifold and divergent.
**Sharmistha Mohanty**, poet, and editor *Almost Island*

There are two kinds of difficult poems. One, which alienate you with their deliberate obscurity. Others, which invite you into a game. A/nil writes the latter kind. His language, wildly allusive, demanding, and whimsical, is not supposed to be parsed into easy intelligible lessons as much as it is supposed to be gotten lost inside of. He is counterintuitive, funny and charmingly esoteric. It is the kind of poetry where you would like to sit with the poet endlessly asking for meanings of this line or that, knowing fully well that he will bewilder you further with his answers.
**Akhil Katyal**, poet and translator

A/nil's poetry is 'the shadow of an inverted rain', unexpected in October, unruly and even uneven, yet affecting all things around. Like he says: 'That which can be said / Must be concealed ... And that which cannot be / Said, must be said at any Prize.'
**M.T. Ansari**, Professor of Comparative Literature, University of Hyderabad

# The Absent Color

a/nil

navayana

*The Absent Color: Poems*
First published by Navayana Publishing Pvt Ltd 2023
Hardback ISBN 9788195539208

10 9 8 7 6 5 4 3 2



With the support of Northwestern | BUFFETT INSTITUTE FOR GLOBAL AFFAIRS

Navayana Publishing Pvt Ltd
155 2nd Floor
Shahpur Jat, New Delhi 110049
navayana.org

Typeset at Navayana in Fournier and Conduit
Printed by Saksham Enterprises, Delhi
Distributed in South Asia by HarperCollins India
Subscribe to updates at navayana.org/subscribe

Amma, Appu, Pappathi, Vennila
This poetry bleeds for you

## Pre Face

In that poetics of decolonization, violence is devioIenced as a psychoanalysis of the subjugated.
It was he who first recognized the cryptic rhetoric of the French nonpolitical thinker.
It is the flayed body.
Violence has two dimensions.
One silences by chopping off the head, while the body remains in its illusory appearance as skin.
The other gives you tongues where the body loses the skin.

Let me be personal.
I have been partially blind from childhood, myopic.
I am partially insighted.
I see through lenses
Which color the world in league with their color.
'To live outside the law, you must be honest.'
'I am not a potentiality for something. I am fully that which I am.'
A lagoon escapes.

There is only desolation around me.
I cry the evening.
It takes the color of my inverted memories.
The point of no return is not a suitable place.
Where suicide is a gesture, death is the game.
I imagine what is left unimagined by all the creators.
I imagine the unimaginable, which as it happens is unmanageable.
'History is a nightmare from which I am trying to awaken.'

Herstory, the correcting fluid, the white solution against the
nightmarish.
A lagoon flows.
There is a cry, far from *The Scream.*
Infantile cry, a beauty, the cry for a space, with fisted arms
for politics.
But where is the cry that cries the death of space?
My mother's womb smelt the flowers of Earth.
They put the flowers, sprang from my mother's womb,
the wounded womb,
On the grave of earth.
And hopes and fists and cries are the remains.
I cry like my earth, the rain of my mother.
Darkling hopes, everywhere, fists in chains.
And my violence and my apologies.

## No Clear Demarcation*

We thus arrive at the fault lines
Of tremor, step by step

Mere repetition, our fears

Earlier, the earth was Euclidean flat
Uncorrupted by mafias
With parallel lines only embracing
Beyond the field of vision

Now neatly Riemannian
Curved, explorable manifolds,
On the surface, all parallel lines,
Once untouched and untouchable,
Coalescing against our vacant eyes

* From Ezra Pound's *Canto XLV*

## Chameleons and Skulls: Two Russian Scenes

The intensity of skulls
reminds me of Eisenstein films
I don't know why
Perhaps they give you
The infinite possibilities of montage

And now
Let us examine
Their first presence
Indeed, it had been before chameleons
How beautiful they were—
Radiating like the sun

And later
Pushed by tectonic movements
They went under, over which grew
Chameleons, the blood suckers
Have you ever traced the taproot of chameleons?
They are in the skulls, in the deep

And now
What is their state
Dark like the Dark Age
With died-out eye-embers
Amidst empty bottles and wastes
Awaiting their destiny

### Scene 1, or how Eisenstein failed

Skulls uproot the taproots
Skulls climb up the Odessa steps
One by one, for no one

Skulls followed by chameleons
Skulls, afraid to death, surrendering

### Scene 2, or what Tarkovsky saw

From Solaris, earth reminds us of earth
New is everything, new York, new Delhi

Long take tapering into a gaze

Blood from the hollow eyes of skulls
Blood from the open mouths of skulls
Blood from the widened eyes of skulls
Blood blackens, earth like earth-skulls

October sky pales over us, for ever*

* Al Stewart, "Roads to Moscow".

## Rebus

The Icarians flight minus More
With utopia for the present

Cabals in flagrante

The suburban Jew-hater
After the metamorphosis
From pure insanity still got it wrong

Neither usura nor avarice
But sinthome's metastasis

What then is the agalma

We believe in God like we believe in money
But when we get down to brass tacks
God cannot be trusted like money

The Buddha and his dhamma
And Ambedkar is well in Kekulé's dream

## Habiru

Rainwards
Glides the smooth flow of the balloon of desires
Sliced from prehistory
Barred with words
No synthesis, just disjunctive
But always
The sky of event emeralds over our despair
We move
Like habiru
Or do we?
We still
Unlike habiru
Or do we?

## Light Shadows

The waxed real
Paralyzed over the Shulamith-like
Added into the mirror–in
Of that which is not
The lips bring tears to the eyes
The threshold of my despair
Is a token of river bounty
Where is the time of promise
In the beginning or the end

The end ends in the middle
Already and always

## Anaclasis

*(In gratitude to A.V. Koshy for a subtle lesson)*

After all
They are just…

No, that is too much of exertion

Like
Millipedes bathed in ink…

No, I don't like them, the traces left

Soul nests

~~I am what I am not~~
Plucking neck-laces

Black
Marks walking, analogously

His
Eventual death discrete digitus

While the Sun raped the lungs of the lake

To have my revenge on them
I will bring a storm river

Sans its cold

## Ode to René

*(Dedicated to Chengu, the most impulsive defender of rational thinking if there ever was one!)*

By the time the Red Venus of Mauern sends the final whore
for Eleusis
And the solitary owl in Neuburg an der Donau succumbs
To the force-field of multitudinous silent death waves
I will have been paired with you in the bluest of manners,
tooth and a/nil

A pairing, not to send a collection of wheels and levers
(You said so, right?
Or did not my memory serve me right as usual?),
But to send your pure spirit in a form clear as crystal

Bit by bit, for me to save it bit by bit
In digital form, for me to delete it bit by bit

I am not sunburning you in your grave
Nor am I making fun of you as I did with others after you
I am damn serious, like a child lost in thought
And all I have to say is this: big time!

The earth is supremely indifferent to the human race that
breathes burden into earth
With insubstantial plastics which will not leave her till she dies
Let the plastic eat us, sculpting our flesh and blood

We shall all be plastic and insubstantial; we will melt in the
fire and be

The world secretes a glueyness like honey
It honeys you even when you repeat the prophets

## Of Poets and Rapists

The spectres of bloodshed lurk in every turn of the tongue
Not pointing to things out there but in our field of vision…

They seem to be pro/positions

In the/rapists, more than anyone else
The eyes are most hawkish for the details

Peeled-off, poetry bleeds

## Fluid Flows

when the lands purloined
move in your freight trains
then stationed
in alien palpitations
of web desires

my love turns
into the unnameable
of my holding-onto

Buttoned-up
ashes with ashes
the sky-dreams
self
divide

## Eyes on the Edge

Every time, in passing, under the moonlit summer sky
Rock-strewn with clouds, you called him in your music
And he answered you in the most musical of manners

In the indelible silence there is

## Oedipus's Briefings

### Before

My eye-lights, echoing the light of the Sun God
Through the constricted fears tapering into you

Penetrating
Sticking

You, like the dead, remained stony yet tepid
Adiabatically inaccessible from my cold Thebes
The kingdom of our wanton youth, fuming

### After

I am open to what surrounds me, the clearing
My blindness touches everything and voids
And I no longer stumble about as I feared

Everything
Nothing

Life, this is more than enough, and I thank you
You have taken me back to the arms of the God

## The Unnameable

In the blueprint, the metaphors,
Born of stupor, remained homeless,
Working nomadically to the black-wholic
Outside the unwashed lips of antiquity
For the interiority of the endless atemporal
Retreat into self annihilation beyond verse

## Summer Rain

Together we fetched rain from the sky
And drew in the fragrance of the earth

Primordial yet every year new

The summer lightning, unlike the sun's hue
Revealed only the essential

Patchy shadows of dances against the sky

The wind was just enough, unable to be blown bare
The sensual aroma of champa and langilangi

Arm in arm we rained in many and many

## Refracted Question

Nothing, the question was
One, two, three
Symmetry of innocence

But time posits asymmetry in intervention
One can be prepared for the future
One cannot in anticipation of the past

One more point
The triangle becomes
A perfect square

Square on the head, to sharpen
The proverbial nail

Everything changes
With nothing changed

To be or not to be
That is not the question

It solves the future in the present

The question is

What is the shape of the question that is past?

## And Why the Other with a Capital O?

Here is
Before I am
Deeply enmeshed in death
Without beyond

The petrified abyss
Ready to send its love
To lives lived a bit at a time
Recorded a bit at a time
When its love sends…

Willing scratches here and there
Leaving holes in the medium of life
Here and there
Erasing the consistency, the data
Which no alcohol wash can retrieve

While in the holographic memory
Lights in different angles
At the same site will reverse
The wisdom of the German philosopher

## As Though

This now between the cry and the laugh is yours
When change does not immobilize the sense

The extinguished, the illusion

Too far my flight after departuring from me
Spiralling down, like a vulture, on to the quarry

The solitary in the solitude

Over the fragrance of the geometric
Severe is the authentic of that ontic

Face is mortality

Hence

You

&

I

## Deep Past

> Only one thing remained reachable, close and secure amid all losses: language. Yes, language. In spite of everything, it remained secure against loss. But it had to go through its own lack of answers, through terrifying silence, through the thousand darknesses of murderous speech. It went through. It gave me no words for what was happening, but went through it. — Paul Celan

Long ago
In the insurmountable silence and aloneness
Of my homeless nights
I always came back to you
In search of a dialogue
I talked to you over and over
In desperation, in delirious fever
You gave me no answers
A shadow outside language
Homeless within language, nothing

That was when I thought I would paint you in watercolour
And I did it in black and red
Incarcerating you in hexagonals, many
The portrait behind the television
Raised many eyebrows
One day I overheard mother telling an aunt
"He is a poet whose family was finished in Hitler's time"
Coincidence, I let your portrait perish
And calmly watched over my growing

Inability at painting
Till she wrote in her poem
That she wanted to see love in my always trembling hands
On the one hand, there is nothing
On the other, there is trembling

Unseen tears disburdening
One thing still missing

## It Slips like Flux but Late

It was then it was never
To be
Always, the same
No more treachery

Crystal violets
Poised to dry up life
And then
Fear, like a pond in winter night

You looked from the depth
Of wars fought, unheroic
You took
Me into your dream's withering

October sky sad as ever
The pale blue, yellow madness
And the red
Clear cry over the mountains

The bird of shadow
Still hovers over depressing sands
For ever
The evening falls

## I Can Only Give You This Refrain*

I am not a poet like me
Nothing is complete for now
Even now is in the middle
Like a Bible without punctuation
Only the clergy would put
Commas and periods and chapter headings
Where there is none
There is emptiness
Void erected by overcoming
The plenitude that is not mine

---

* From Robin Shirley's translation of François Villon's poem "Ballade des Dames du Temps Jadis"

## Immobile Eternity

Gradually the whore evolves
Into the loci
Of the blue-eyed prince

Still void…

Two different flowers
En passant
Silence awaiting hope is pure
Violence divine

So humid is the letter
Where we die

## Lebensraum

Which colour, the soul-organ
this en-holding
I of eye is then driven
in the offing

Do the birds have becoming-solitude?
Or just yoke, yearning and multitude?

## Habakkuk

Lips in the unguarded time
Not yet swollen by the bite
On a kissable road
Wrestled antediluvian colossi

Filled with infinite love
And the aporia of a sudden joy
Holding the face closer to the lips
A bite back?

"I love you" in the lessest audible
"That is only for you, don't tell others"
Only women are capable of such depth
Moment for infinity, untimely rather

The dead do not lie
That's why we call them the dead

## Memoirs of a Woman of No Importance

The rhythms burst asunder
Deceiving the lineaments
Her flesh

Stoned inside

~~Mother~~ still calling
When the kestrels come home to roost

No rest in inconsistencies, the peeled off skin,
The noodle brain, the blood of not-menses,
The nail that pierced, yet not nail,

Swim in

I, you have my her much offended

Far off
The vanished

Release them

~~Time~~

## I Admire the Genius

No joke it was
Yet laughter echoed on the other side
Of the river
Till it spiralled into pure interiority
Of rejection, silence
Split into seconds
Then minutes, hours
Days, calendar years

Sobs of being caught in pain
Night after night, in solitude

Durée, the unsaid of my tongue
And the least understood

## The Dance of Darkness

All things are full of weariness beyond uttering. The eye is not satisfied with seeing, nor the ear filled with hearing. That which has been is that which shall be; and that which has been done is that which shall be done: and there is no new thing under the sun. (Ecclesiastes: 1: 8–9)

Every flower
As the Japanese have correctly surmised
Is the dance of darkness
A smile to the sun
Rooted firmly in the earth
That's how the dancer becomes
The Buddha knew it
Once he was a lion
He had terrible memory
And died of dysentery
Body painted white
That's its technique
There you see darkness
Now you travel
It's no nonsense
The stars are just traces
Fusions which could evaporate millions
But then you know
In my childhood, in the front yard
On a mat we would all lie
And sing and sing
I would count the stars

And think it was all real
Years later
They are still there
So unreal
Because we don't know
If they are still there
Like a china pot in the outer space

The valetudinary state of the universe
The universe has a migraine

## Pure Difference

Embodied failure
Is a machine

An essence, a being
A no becoming

Sans
Love
It is always elsewhere

Sans
Sex
is a failed encounter

Sans
Karuna
a figure of speech

In its essence
Unchanging
With desire
As substance
The machine
Of machines

Long ago
Beckett knew
The destiny

Of becoming
Man, despite
His Nobel Prize

## Peniel

> To restore silence is the role of objects.
>
> Samuel Beckett, *Molloy*

Your chlamys, obtrusive,
With hidden distance below
Forms imaginary lines to infinity
As in Renaissance painting
At the end of each one finds
Springs, firm
But not visible to the I
In order that perfect symmetry
Between the face and the invisible
Is brought into Being

So many words still, trapping…

## Survivor of Loneliness

Rhapsody of the unfolded
Over the night
The sound recedes into infinity
Red-shifted
Now here beyond through
Crumbling everything

## Querencia

*(to Reuel's father)*

Never knew it would come to this
Assured, this moment, it seems,
Of your verse of my vomiting blood
Yet its glory is never mine, always

I-ed by you and eyed by you again
My impossibility in your voluptuousness

## James Joyce's Onan

You were finished in a book of poems
Like a worm ending up on a watery hook.
Within it only gruesome rhyme
That cannot seize the burden of your look.

In the struggle for the perfect non-be of life
In the temporal, beyond the beyond of space
All that is needed is the sharpness of a knife
Piercing the content going beyond the phrase.

Hence
This
You
O
O
O
O
O
.

A

M

A

R

## Entre Nous

In alterity we can find an enemy
That's cool, perfect, yet difficult
As if consenting to horror
One can forgive many people
But there are some people it is difficult to forgive
It is difficult to forgive you

### Over Seventy Thousand Fathoms of Water

You the sky incarnate
Pick snow from the furnace
And throw it coolly
At the sinews of memories
As the rain brings horror
To the clouds of your hair

I dream of your face
Soft with struggles
Cuddled in my arms

The sun waves and rocks
I brought from the east
And all the surprise was in your eyes
A sigh that I heard clearly
All the way down I felt the pain
Of your nail yet to be born
A new sprout in the backyard
The songs of various birds
The vines of blue bells on the wall
Red red red all the way
Slanting through the white
The first of red with flesh
Not in the vision of the church yet
With your nudity crowd and kid

## Fire Eclipse

It unfolded
When the curled smoke struggled
Toward perching-death
Unsuspected, a flow
And then,
From the icy cool of the mountain
Among the clouds I formed your shape
Abandoned, the river sprang forth
From the tears of my blood
Into the sullen woods
The flower mocks you no more
It withered even before
You said
Where?

a/nil

## The Hate Song of Sand Piper Strong

Years ago
The Norwegian proto-fascist
Did it

In Heideggerian fashion
Into the antediluvian innocence
Of being

Now after so many years
Far from Scandinavian dejection
And its icy waters

In the summer heat
Of an over-grown feudal Palakkad
A sluggish movement

Just as a viper
Trapped
In clear crystal sands of homogeneity

Doing it again
In child-talks of do-goodism
Self violence and reflection

Proving a prey
To Alcoholics Anonymous'
Long-drawn doubts:

Yup, every one of them—
The low-paid lackeys
Of transnational bourgeoisie
It sucks big time

My god, help me
Help this psychopath on the make to be an atheist

The Hegelian rejoinder:
Like the fascists, we believe in god
But unlike them, we don't trust him

What about the rest?
The fellow-combatants
Of Lacan's heir

Those sex-Maoists of French radicalism
Grouped under world association
For a Lacanian orgy?

Well, we know well
The worn-out strategies
Of cold-blooded animals:

Use the sun's heat
And the ambient heat
To regulate your body heat

Ahem
Does cold-blooded murder
Evoke our reptilian past?

## When Hegel, Bearded, Gently Fights for the Guerrillas

Every failed gonza Zappa
Minus acid sex
Musical Wittgenstein and philosophical Schoenberg
Cupids of melancholy on pubis angelical

Meanwhile
Marx, clean-shaven,
Reads *Wall Street Journal* and kisses Jenny and the tea
Like they do in the ads, faithful hubby
Beware; it is a sign of God:
Karl will pull out the Capital
From Dalal Street when the market is hot
In Alimuddin Street Max Hardcore overworked
To bail out a nation ravaged by inflation and Ashis Nandy

On a rainy evening in Thrissur
When night falls on the certified civilization
Far away from death and mountain
Much humidity

## Recess

The whisky fossilized; nothing.
A drink from heaven
Would cost the heart pressed on the trigger.
Waiting is poetry.
I read poems from the book of December
And leaped; heaven is black and cold.
I do love dying
Only if you won't consider my sacrifice, darling.

## The Couple

On the rock(s) bottom
Imperial is the waiting
In the tremors of flayed bodies
Void, essentially
While things emerge
In the violence of cosmic imbalance

Of love

The universe is so perfect
That not even G-d can set it right

## Unplannable Supplement

Lips survive the butt-ends
A process in time nouned
And futured in the ash bin
While in all the gin-joints of time
The gin in cut glass, long after
The mad demise of dirty boy
Retains its clarity, the glass
Mirroring the mirror which
Mirrors the clarity of history

It's my turn, I realize, to be:
Authentic to the unfolding
And I am polishing the lens
Of the scratched glasses
To have clarity for Eye

Clarity is never an accident

## Birds in the Six World from the Sun

As God recedes into the malls of antiquity
Every skinhead oozes out a serpent
A background radiation of cancerous pricks
In all my leaden lips over my grey flowers
The red-necked roads in fire crackers

Too late you are my Milada Horáková
Every poet has to sing gallows throat-out
A nation in every medium walks in
Progressive jazz man and here we have
Three colors in the color spectrum

The sad alcohol burns in the dance of rain
While the red of menses thickens in the street

## Anxiety Neurosis Anonymous

**The problem:**

It seems…
How shall I put it…
Coming as I am from…
I mean… from a land of blue ink…
The trees here… they are plenty…
They give off carbon dioxide…
There is so much suffocation here…

**The solution:**

Let me put things as they are
If what you have said is true
Let me act as soon as possible
We will call a meeting first
Let us buy some banyan trees and plant them here
The CM says they give oxygen in abundance
Let it be so because he knows things
Buddha was enlightened under the same tree
Let us get slightly enlightened

## The Silent Presence

My silence
Stalks your shadow
Unobtrusively

Even your shadow
Deserves a thorough defense
From every danger

Because it is your shadow

## Tomorrow Wedding

It was a sundown of dreaming
And of the yet to happen before dawn.
The music, the dances, cards and whiskey,
And bottles emptied for cocktail
In the land of my green grass,
Surrounded by cuts innumerable
Where we used to fish with bare arms.
Then you, my infinite content,
Reminded me of the purchase,
In a duct where you found
A saleswoman about to be married,
Elegant in a sari from the eighties,
Very dark, beautiful, wide eyes fluttering,
Hair falling, like a black rainbow from the sky,
Well educated for a six-year-old,
Who thought she was more educated
Than mother, his mother who taught him poetry,
For she was more beautiful than his mother.

And then
The limousine, all white, came into
The glittering of our lightless joy
With anguished eyes, we watched, like clowns,
The headlights went off, darkness all around
We could only hear the cry of an engine withdrawing.
Again it came, did the same,
But stopped by our dim light.
He, in his business-like tone, said

He had a present for the wedding.
It was her, the one at whom my daughter never smiled,
Unmoving, wrapped, a gift.
Excited, we asked him
Why he hadn't stopped the first time.
He was not sure if he was invited, he said.
I was so happy that she was there.
We did not even notice that she came from the dead,
We did not care she was a thing.

I was so happy, so happy,
That I danced.
You, as only you could do, sensed me,
Climbed deep,
Felt it,
And said, rejoicing,
We won't go shopping tonight.

## The Journey of the Rejected

The black of her eyes in the horizon
Before the singularity
Beyond which is the torn upside down
Moving spring/body does not signify movement
Nor does it change
It repeats the unrepeatable

## A Alegria do Povo

A brave new world was born
In the crooked legs' feral dance
A fer-de-lance
Baroque bizarre
Yet an angel of the poet
And his sister's brown bird

Neither east nor west
But over the cuckoos' nests
Into the singularities of virtual time
Of alcohol of loneliness
The Combines
Couldn't bend the unknown death

The absolute artist of the feutbol-arte
At Maracana with frozen limbs
What did those limbs want?
The empty space of the enemy's goal
Or the birds in the Brazilian wilderness?
Far above, God still plays dice.

## Good-for-nothing Ugly Duckling

Star, rarely, stops
This abyss, and it
Before it, cleaving
Striving for worth
Into the bottomless
The shadow, mine
Strikes like thunder
Forever passing, oh
Then forever silent
Like the leaves
Of Asparagus, green
Releases itself the
Impossible of color
Vanished history
Altered landscape
The sea infiltrated
Memory, only thus
We are that
Prison of shadows
Shadow of prisons
Both ways works it
Shadows criss-
Crossing, what the
Hell, when prison
Is meandering up
The mountain, from
Which springs the
Life's remote beyond

Rarely do we see the
Sun hang on the hair
Where there is winter
There is winter, and
Water spring follows
Without Spirit, it is
For itself, ultimately
The time will tell
Because time has no
Tongue to speak
Speak like a woman
Hysteric over Barbie
Doll images and fancy
Dress, we are our own
Dogs, since, there is
No fact to memorize
Only factories, where
They cook catfish on
Acid induction cooker
To serve the dogs that
We are, inner organic
Its movement, unity
Nothing else in the
Lonely night when one
Strips oneself of
Like how many times
Will it cease to be
Real, this self-loving

There is no method
Even in madness, the
Self-closed nudity is
Miserable, when the
Space itself is crammed
With times uncertain
Of which only memory
Fashions what is most
Decaying in the world
That which can be said
Must be concealed, for
We suspect clarity is
Possible only in the abyss
When life is suspended
And that which cannot be
Said, must be said at any Prize,
that is when dogs bark,
and the caravan moves,
everyone solitary
In the crowd of home-
Lost, when movement
Aches for the trigloo.

## The Castle

Past the objet d'art in the sieve
Fortified with internal damnation
I walked the days

Memory is a rising damp of flesh and blood

Like a flash
The timeless within a second

Later I sat beside my sister
Looking at the clear water
Of October evenings

My Infinite crystal

I fished the worlds
She washed the words

## Gleaning in Bethlehem

A Moabite
She smelled of barley at his feet on the threshing floor
In the days when judges ruled

She left her country her people
To follow an intolerant god
To a foreign country

A sleep, a bodily passion
That cut through the flesh of levirate marriage
And every one became an exile once again

David to Jesus
Outsiders within the vortex of certainty
For women gain justice only in relation to men

## The Absent Color

Death is the moment of siesta
When the eve drops climb up the sierra.
I need your kisses badly.
I still love the things that were once gold:
The flowers, colorful and odorous,
Walk alone in the misty field,
The sun between the two peaks,
The milky moon.

I still write poetry
And nothing happens; customary glance.
Where is that leonine poise?
In the repository we read countless names
Unknown to our childish knowledge.
The photograph was not there,
Nor the piercing cries.

Either faces and no face
Or faces without names.

## Imagining October

Poetry brings nothing except black.
It moves along the yellow pages
Till mother wakes me into slumber.
She,
The astral substance of my song,
Perfects art,
Holding together the pieces,
Words, boughs, spirit, spine
Crushed
Beneath the severe heaviness
Of multiple gravities.
No éclat for the real act.

## The Hexagonal Casement

Geranium flouts the rules of the game
The musical smell of potpourri
Watches westward medley
Cyclone, the whore, and the child
Twirl the dusts of the brick road
A limousine
Can break through the wrinkled pain
Of animal passion
That is the mystery of it
The lines on zebra
And zebra lines are same
In all possible universes
Until blood dries up in the linctus
No one ever left this room piqued
No world for sleuthing
Hardly a memory prison
A wind in blue, a masquerade
There is an oubliette
Where broken languages are preserved
With a door sealed with tongues of poison
Why the room and street
The vast blue itself is otiose

## The Last Drop of Blue

Resentment shadows in the bleak tower,
Where I dream of nothing but flower.
The winds of colors absent in thee hover
Till all the dark is dripping and over.

My night surmises the legends of wars fought.
Differing opinions; nothing leftover except naught.
Or that the sharp shingles are bought
From the hazy market where love is sought.

You are the death that is you,
And here I, the last drop of blue.

## The Night and Blindness of 98

It had been over before I cried

Grand call from the abyss
Like the shadow of an inverted rain
In the imminence of shine.

## Few Pages from the Rain of Thrissur

You came pony-tailed
Gathering buttercups from swift August.
I watched the pungent drops
Ooze from the pores of your skirt
Adorned with green flowers, light and big,
On frightening white.

The outpour persisted as long as it persisted—
Colorless from the deep, the firmament.
The coffee you gave me was excellent,
Black, sour and saccharine.
I polished the shoes; silence
And fluttering eyes and shivering lips.

With a sigh towered into the depths
The drops left over from the sky bounty
Dipped ripples of flare on the streamy face.
Across the meadow the hills seemed
Pale as your young breasts; yet
Colorful, clean, and sad.

The soft touch flooded with future blows.
The immensity of monsoon drops on the blade,
Bleeding into a thousand mirrors
That reflected the swift guns from others.
The rainbow floored itself into
The curly hair, the rich of Parisian perfume.

The bricks aired the silence of madness.
Of all the memories in the world
The memory of a ruthless flutter survived
In the antique store; we melted in a parting kiss.
Shanties echoed from distant shores
As our cosmic bodies distorted a cry.

## The Principle Rule

An avalanche of remembrance to the migraine of history
A long void and terrible despair
As of leaves falling from the final tree.

## Declaration of Independence

We must
Before we get sterilized for good on acid stoves
On which they had cooked cat fish
Strive for the singular and maintain
Our right to have no rights
Like so many times before in failures...
Because, contrary to the professed,
It is not the living but the extinct
That are to be accommodated
And also the yet to be born
Between two nonentities
We are chromosomes exposed
To some silent stellar collapse
Inwardly, like the death before death.
But the irony, if the word has not lost its significance,
Is that the universe still is expanding
Every galaxy moves away from the other
Like the colored dots on an expanding balloon

## Pappathi

Trapped in your hair
The cloud longing imploded
Raining, with its thunder
Onto your eyelashes,
Infalling into your iris…

In your river water birds flower

## Nostalgia for the Void

In the mazed chaos
We lost our way

The here and now
Was too heavy
With its trenches
Cages grills
Walls paths
And above all
With innocence

But you were a dream
Of ferocious intensity
Amid boring reality

Pure
Like a dew drop
On mountain-top

## Eithor

alas! this state space
when we get rid of the crystals
of soultalk, in slow pace
to attain the details

will crowd together, as in
metastases, the cancerous
jealousied, into air broken thin
with an excess of the amorous

perched at the edge of signal
the unformed shapes of men
burst out two-bodied model
digging holes in performed den

where our inward love and loathe
always, already shadowed in the wall
endow us with grapes of wrath
unmoved, even in a journey beyond goal

still caveman
the philosuffer
the profetter

~~much, much, this exo-construct~~
~~of dry stones~~

## Final Consolation

There you have it,
Bound, the ether horizon
Of your corolla signalling
The wordless of the world

That point, without spectre
We reach, always-mine, long before
We embark on a journey unto
You, fleeing the soul-map

The red, like a star of yesteryears,
Sticks to our eyes a present, an unmoving
While the white splashes bloom
Below parabolically without fixity

Those soft water boughs, untrimmed, will
As it—oh—goes by, haunt our illusive landscapes and
One day, the birds perching on the infinite waves
Singleleggedly against the currents will
Teach us to be precise with our emotions
And then we will mourn the loss
Of that which we never possessed

## Peopled Night

Old, almost perished

Night howls the wild trees, dancing
Leaves falling, visible only in lightning
Unsupported by thunder, raining

Dusty, almost unbreathable

Near the window, clayed
I look for something familiar
To cling to, amidst the terror
And the loneliness of eyes,
Like the smell of my mother
Or, even more, the smell
Of her stomach when I put
My arms around her, as a kid,
To kiss her soft velvety bubble—
Traces of the pregnant days
Marked on the skin, a sign
Of separation, of the Real

In the darkness I hear what I had to
For in my darkness only sound is visible;
Penetrates

Cough, familiar! with
Past imprinted, pleurisy smelling of
Sick rooms, adjoining corridors

That are damp, stuffy and semi-dark

Near the window, grilled
I grope for something recent
The touch of a kid's watch-hand
Hoping time would dissolve there
And with it, the world glued
To me, and with it, the me
Glued to the world, unsticking
My tongue tastes the salty
Tears, infinite crystals, waiting
For their anti-matters, at a less miserable
Time, a journey without beginning,
From without, to where already is

Rain starts bringing tremor from the sky
And becoming me:
Inside yet beyond, always already
Night, terribly dark
Storm, ferocious intensity
Trees, wild dancing ready to break
Sky, hopelessly grey in darkness
Leaves, non-beings without thoughts
Earth, indifferent to its own cry
Tiger, backtracking, deadly
Grass, dry as ever over red soil

Rain, rain, rain…

Stops.

## The Night Has Tenderness

Smooth, ephemeral
The skin shapes the moment

Only you can
Sustain the beneath-the-void
Of life
This life

When my nest implodes into
The serene wilderness of your skyline

… a dream within a dream within a dream …

You, upright, outside

Then

Withered, space
Receded, time

Still, still outside

You

The night has the tenderness to be alone
When I touch your face
Smooth, ethereal

## Unremembered

drag we from
the pack of wolf
men before
the empty page
destines you
eviscerated and
smelling of the
corolla dangling
in the winter wind
the nail split and
blood oozing
repeats a walk
in the street
arm in arm, a
gaze spilling over
to your flesh wound
merges with the
yellow flowers
on the move

## Mountain Fire

Among the clouds over mountains
I saw you
Imploding into the fragrance of rain
The rainbow of your smell
Slowly
Spreading its wings into the tremors
Of what has been
Suturing
Different planes
Wounds
Pains
Into a balmy calmness
As I drove past the rough edges
Of a road gone mad

## Mourning in Error

few hours' drive from his eventual
plunge into madness
the poet, perched atop a mountain
and shrouded by clouds pitch black

going noward
conjured up, without end
menstrual flowers on the bare boughs
of a lonely tree silhouetted by

a sky that lost its sky-color
in a final attempt to ease
the cramps that his mother
felt light years ago

curling into a ball of tears
on a rainy day, on a pointed rock
her nails piercing the lower abdomen
to fish out the cysts in her womb

inner-inverted from the scary ashes
the blueprint of smoke rings
elucidate the deepest passion
of the beginning

so tortuous
is the temporal
the letter
and its destination

## The Protocol of the Pass

ash-canned on the event horizon
by sailors on a trip to splinters
this we of yesteryears was thrown
like a piece of animal protein
to the hyenas, whose staccato laughter
leaves untouched the epiphany of flesh
while
the eye of yesterday's kiss
which wept sweetly the fragrance of earth
sketches the spectral splash of oars

along the sur-face
a cry deep-blue

like the moon's, the crown red
in velvety wine, did in its slumber

## Scholium

Place it above all memories
The least understood
And beget the red moon

Flee, flee this evil

We embrace a language forlorn
Racer-sharp, inflated
And this sadness produces things imperfect

Flee, flee this evil

Recollect the spontaneous silence of the body
The winged horse
And exclude substance

Flee, flee this evil

## Not yet a Vanishing Mediator

Neither arnica nor eyebright
But just mountains, mountains

Yet the breeze of your generous heart!

Those soft pale sisterly hands!
So lean, so fragile
Yet strong enough to hold an entire world
Unshaken, till your death
The valley, the green meadow, the pranks, the wild run,
  your fluttering eyes
The untimely dance, the song, repetition, infinite nothingness,
  you, you, you

I searched in vain for the red eyes
The aura of a pang, of extreme loneliness,
Of a wound planted inside the skull
Long before we met as sister and brother

The sign
Only my myopic eyes can see
On your forehead
And mine
Only your myopic eyes can see
On my forehead

This is more than enough
To bind me closer and closer to you.

## For Ever the Dust

The stamped multiples, exhausted.

Like many men before me
I set the sky well above me
But setting the void is another thing

One-more-less
And still one
And still
And
An
A

## Vennila

Sunrays
Into the heart of the stream
Transfixing the tiny lifeworld
You
Weave colours around
The musical mood

## Flayed

Splash
The anxious waves of silkiness
In the river Sacrifice

The roving, soft, rhythmic
Hands hang on to
The breeze
Evaporate the skin
Bit by bit
You melt
Red overflows
Two leaves ashore
Rustle

## The Exchange Sacrifice

Suddenly suddenly

Like a fragrance-storm against the skin vortex
Of your non-aroundness
Brother hell, like the vanishing mediator
Slipped into the event horizon

Disappeared just like that
Knew this before, and hence
Prepared with drained eyes—
Goodbye—no turn back to a second call

Years ago, with my mother on the sandy beach
I plucked two pigeons' salt
Oh, they smelled of blue deep
Mother warned: they go back, always

And they did, like always
Blood stained, torn apart, feathers here and there
Death, flight-back, and inward guilt
Of being there

Not necessarily in that order

## Post-truth Whiskey-shot

The night street lit in flames, fuming
With ripples of black smoke soaring high
Drunk, with downcast eyes straight on the sweat-hut
From twenty-four feet above the brick road
A scream, and then, a blast
Oh...
Was it that young lady
No, no lady, a young girl full of, what shall I say
Lady desire.
Short, dark, round.
Swollen fingers, toes dirty.
A woman.
No! a girl still with black hair, black eyes and black skin
Who visited black magic.
Untouchable was your food.
A beggar? A maid? A beggar-made?

Next morning
As roasted matter mixed with molten fabric
Was slowly gliding downwards, defying the ice-stillness
Of the pond of December, a blood-red water
The boy in the restaurant,
With trepidation, took hold of my hands
Tiny fingers, tiny palms,
Made dirty by soot-labor
And whispered in an unknown tongue
Then translated as
"Sir, I always wanted to study."

And cried and cried
Searching in my hands for the magic of words.
Head in my breast
Fingers in his hair.
I knew never would I cry again.

## O, Those White Streaks!

At first, a body without head
In an amphitheatre of the unknown
A mask in place of the face
Red red plastic
Covering my face with a towel
I cried and cried
Once the veil of tears was lifted
You emerged clearly
Post-surgical, memory torn off
Blood oozing, stains on the cotton
Your face with quarter of the head ripped
Whispering without words
Only I knew what it meant
A rage against a silent murder
O, your frantic kisses in my right palm!
Aesthetic, unforgettable
And your complaint, meek:
Only you two godless come to see me
Your favourite son was not around
The big one dangled his legs from the tank

## Mnemosyne

Emcee cash, the belligerent
Ripples of pure leftover
Of our your river, without edges
Can fly, blooded in half widowish
Days after menstruation

Do you know the exact words

Mountains, I know
Meandering paths, I know
I am a son of the farthest North
Ice-scented, broken over rough rocky edges
Heavy, still rolling to gather Moses
Your sea knows only sardine
Empty bottles with German names
And it takes years in water to be like us
Melting melted and still somehow is
Glass made of glass
To pure glas
You—undream

## Rustle Dance

Entrapped
In the curly abundance
Of your thought stream
My wor l ds, stoic
Dull, linear
Break loose
The prison house
To follow the bird-becoming

To the antithetical
Of the now/here

## Without You

Babasaheb
there would have been nothing here for us.

Amminechi, Velliamma, Velliamma(yi)
tears would have been meaningless.

Sreeku, Kuttan chettan, Laila chechi, Babu chettan, Raji chechi,
Mini chechi, Revathi chechi,
Ashokan chettan, Kannan, and Thumbi
the alienation would have been unbearable.

Chengu mash, CB mash, Koshy mash, and Vijayakumar mash
I would have thought that I was into something.

Sister Hell
the wound inside would have gone unnoticed.

Abhi
this would never have seen the light of day.

Anand and Alex
this would have gone unchallenged.

a/nil, A-Nil, A Nil aka Anilkumar Payyappilly Vijayan was born in 1976 in Thrissur, Kerala. He is an Associate Professor of English at Government Arts and Science College, Pathiripala, Palakkad. His doctoral thesis, from Kannur University, "Untouchability of the Unconscious: Containment and Disfigurement of Dalit Identity in Malayalam Cinema", uses Lacanian psychoanalysis to inquire into the construction of Dalit identity in Malayalam cinema.